# Could the myth be true?

There really was a city of Troy. What is left of it was found 100 years ago in Turkey. Some experts think that there probably were wars between the Greeks and the Trojans. However, the wars weren't over the love of a beautiful woman called Helen – the Greeks were much more likely to have been bickering over land and crops!

# ODYSSEUS
## AND THE
# WOODEN HORSE
### *Allan Drummond*

One morning, just like every other morning, the sun rose over the city of Troy. No ships could be seen on the open sea. But there, on the deserted beach, stood a huge wooden horse.

One of the horse's great eyes flickered as a young boy soldier looked out.

"Wake up everybody, it's morning!" It was Odysseus, calling down to his fellow Greek soldiers who were huddled in the hollow body of the horse. "I can see Troy. And the city gates are opening!" he whispered.

Sure enough the great gates of Troy were opening, and great crowds of people came out and wandered down to the beach to look at the huge beast that had suddenly appeared outside their city.

"The Greek army has gone!" they cheered " – And left nothing but this crazy wooden horse."

"It's so big!" shouted one.

"It's a trick," said another, tapping suspiciously at the horse with a spear.

"Beware of Greeks when they offer gifts," said a third. "But who cares? We're free at last!"

In the end the Trojans decided to tie ropes around the monster and haul it up the hill into their city.

"We'll make it a monument to the end of the war!" they cheered.

Inside the horse Odysseus and his men crouched quietly as it bucked and rolled. Odysseus could hardly believe it, his plan was working!

From his tunic he took out a piece of flat, shiny metal and looked at it in the half-dark. On it was a picture of a beautiful girl.

"Helen," he promised her, "by tonight you'll be free."

The timbers of the horse rumbled and roared and Odysseus and his friends could hear the Trojans outside heaving and shouting.

"Hey! Odysseus, when we get to the city will you make us a giant wooden bird and fly us over the walls?" joked one of the soldiers nervously. "Shh!" said Odysseus. "Trust me."

So the dark uncomfortable journey continued and everyone inside the horse had time to think about the years they had spent, and the battles they had fought trying to get into Troy. It was all because of Helen.

Helen had been stolen from the palace of her husband King Menelaus by Paris, the Prince of Troy. So the king ordered his armies from all over Greece to set sail for Troy and rescue her. Odysseus had joined the rescuers' party.

He had thought they could overpower the Trojans easily! But weeks had turned into months and months into years. And although they had fought hundreds of battles, still they camped outside Troy while Helen was a prisoner inside.

Finally, worn out with fighting, the Greek army had almost given up. But then Odysseus had spoken up.

"What we need is a way of getting a few of our best men inside the city gates," he had said. And then he told them of his plans for the Wooden Horse . . .

"Let's do it," they cried. "Count me in!"

Everyone wanted a part of Odysseus's plan.

So the Wooden Horse was built.

Nothing like it had ever been made before. It had a hidden door in its belly, and space inside for thirty men.

The work was done in secret behind a wooden screen, out of sight of the Trojans.

Odysseus made the horse's huge head, and gave its eyes a look of beauty and terror.

And when the work was done, the Greeks took down the screen, set fire to their camp, boarded their ships and sailed away. Then Odysseus and his chosen friends clambered into the horse's hollow belly.

And now the day had come. Huddled together, the young soldiers were thrown from side to side as the Trojans dragged the great beast up the hill, through their gates and into the very centre of their city.

Odysseus' plan was working!

The Trojans sang and danced around the horse, happy that they could live in peace at last.

Night fell and the Trojans stumbled into their beds. Silence fell around the wooden horse, which stood garlanded with wreaths and flowers.

But there was one person in the city who did not sleep that night.

It was Helen, in her high prison tower, looking down on the huge wooden horse.

"This is a trick," she thought to herself, for she was a Greek and knew the ways of the Greeks. "All I have to do now is wait."

The city slumbered peacefully under
a bright moon, and when all was deadly
quiet the secret trap-door in the horse's
belly opened. Down fell a rope ladder,
and down the ladder crept Odysseus
and his men.

They tiptoed to the city gates, killed the sleeping sentries, and heaved open the massive doors. Troy was now an open city.

Down by the beach, under the moon, the Greek ships were waiting. The Greek soldiers waded ashore and swarmed up through the great gates into the city. They were ready for battle!

And what a battle it was. Troy was ablaze and ten long years of war were over in one terrible night of killing.

The flames spread to Helen's tower but she was
saved in time and taken to the fleet of waiting ships.
    And with her went the Greek soldiers, proud of
Odysseus and his clever plan, but above all happy
to be returning home at last.

Odysseus had to leave his wooden horse behind him.
Some say the horse caught fire and burnt that night in the
terrible flames. But others swear they saw it – still standing
tall and strong – as the sun came up over the ruins of Troy.

*for Jamie
with thanks*

Orchard Books
96 Leonard Street, London EC2A 4RH
*Orchard Books Australia*
14 Mars Road, Lane Cove, NSW 2066
ISBN 1 85213 723 1 (hardback)
ISBN 1 86039 103 6 (paperback)
First published in Great Britain 1995
First paperback publication 1996
© Allan Drummond 1995
The right of Allan Drummond to be identified as the Author
and as the Illustrator of this work has been
asserted by him in accordance with the
Copyright, Designs and Patents Act, 1988.
A CIP catalogue record for this book is available from the British Library.
Printed in Belgium

The story of how the Greeks tricked the Trojans using a giant wooden horse is full of exciting imagery, so it was great fun working out how the words and pictures should go together.

To get started I had to decide just how big the wooden horse should be. One of my first rough sketches was of Odysseus and his men hiding inside the horse. This gave me the scale I needed and led me to ask myself what it would be like to actually be inside the statue. How could you peep out and spy on the enemy? Perhaps through the horse's eyes... This is how my ideas grew.

I looked at pictures on the very oldest Greek pots as a guide to how the soldiers should look, and then I relied on my own excitement and imagination – and your imagination too – for the rest.

**Allan Drummond**